Uh-oh, Cleo

Underpants ON MY Head

Jessica Harper

ILLUSTRATED BY
Jon Berkeley

G. P. Putnam's Sons

G. P. PUTNAM'S SONS

A division of Penguin Young Readers Group.

Published by The Penguin Group.

Penguin Group (USA) Inc., 375 Hudson Street, New York, NY 10014, U.S.A. Penguin Group (Canada), 90 Eglinton Avenue East, Suite 700, Toronto, Ontario M4P 2Y3, Canada (a division of Pearson Penguin Canada Inc.). Penguin Books Ltd, 80 Strand, London WC2R 0RL, England. Penguin Ireland, 25 St. Stephen's Green, Dublin 2, Ireland (a division of Penguin Books Ltd.). Penguin Group (Australia), 250 Camberwell Road, Camberwell, Victoria 3124, Australia (a division of Pearson Australia Group Pty Ltd). Penguin Books India Pvt Ltd, 11 Community Centre, Panchsheel Park, New Delhi - 110 017, India. Penguin Group (NZ), 67 Apollo Drive, Rosedale, North Shore 0632, New Zealand (a division of Pearson New Zealand Ltd.). Penguin Books (South Africa) (Pty) Ltd, 24 Sturdee Avenue, Rosebank, Johannesburg 2196, South Africa. Penguin Books Ltd, Registered Offices: 80 Strand, London WC2R 0RL, England.

Design by Richard Amari. Text set in Eco 101.

Library of Congress Cataloging-in-Publication Data

Harper, Jessica. Underpants on my head / Jessica Harper ; illustrated by Jon Berkeley.
p. cm. "Uh-oh, Cleo." Summary: When Cleo and her family go on vacation, they experience a freak August snowstorm while hiking on Mt. Baldy. [1. Hiking—Fiction. 2. Vacations—Fiction. 3. Family life—Fiction.] I. Berkeley, Jon, ill. II. Title.
PZ7.H231343Un 2009 [Fic]—dc22 2007039268   ISBN 978-0-399-24672-2

1 3 5 7 9 10 8 6 4 2

Chapter 1

Two things you hardly ever see are snow in summer and underpants on my head. But if you'd been on Mount Baldy last August 19th, you'd have seen both at once!

I kind of hope that was your last chance.

It all started when we flew out west for our family vacation. Here's what we brought: three car seats, eight suitcases, five backpacks and Mom's Super Bag. (Plus two parents and six kids.)

When we squeezed past the flight attendant to get to our eight seats, she counted us and her eyebrows popped up. If she knew our last name, she'd have laughed her head off, like everyone does: "Bah, hah! The Small family! You gotta be kiddin' me!"

Quinn hated it when Mom buckled him in next to her. "Yah! Yah! Yah! Yah!" he shouted.

I was going to sit behind Quinn, but Jenna barged past me and plopped her *Harry Potter* down on the seat I wanted.

"I get the window!" she said, all loud, like she was barking.

"Mom said I could, since I get carsick." I tried not to sound a hundred percent crabby.

"This isn't a car." Jenna fastened her seat belt.

"I mean motion sick, Jenna. You *know* what I mean," was what I said. *Miss Boss of the World*, was what I thought. Already that day she: 1) made ME feed Lucy, our dog, which is HER job, but SHE was "too busy." And 2) she jammed a bunch of HER stuff in MY suitcase, so now it was a big bursting

3

mess. Plus, 3) she made me put HER snacks and water in MY backpack, so she'd have room in hers for HER precious *Harry Potter*.

"Just chew gum," Jenna said. She settled in and got busy reading.

"Cleo, take the other window," Dad said,

but Jack already had that seat behind Jenna. "Let's go, Jack, scoot over." Dad was carrying Lily and Ray (who's Quinn's twin) and his backpack and he was almost as crabby as me.

"Awwwwww." Jack took about a year and half to move to the aisle seat.

When I squished past him to sit down, he handed me a throw-up bag. "Here you go, Barf Girl."

Dad plunked Lily down next to Jenna and sat with Ray behind me and Jack. Ray was chewing on a tractor. He flipped a switch that made the tractor play "The Farmer in the Dell." He switched it off, he switched it on, over and over while he chewed.

"Yah! Yah! Yah! Yah!" Quinn wouldn't stop. Mom pulled his purple spider toy from the Super Bag, but Quinn just threw it all wild, like babies do. It flew over Mom and hit the old guy across the aisle, *smack*, right on his bald head. He made a loud noise that sounded like "GOPHER!"

"Whoa, jeez, sorry about that, terribly sorry." Dad tried to apologize, but the bald guy just flapped open his newspaper and stuck his face in it.

Jenna was so busy reading, she missed the whole thing. She was gone, in wizard

land. She didn't even hear Lily next to her playing Bears-and-Barbie. Lily's blond Barbie was whining at the pocket-size Bear Family:

"What will I do without my magic shoelaces?!"

"Oh, Mrs. Kleenex, we will save you from the bad dragon!" Papa Bear said in Lily's low Papa voice.

Jenna kept reading, right through all the whining and growling. I think she could read *Harry Potter* even if her pants were on fire.

I like to read too, but I'm not interested in all those wizard books. I'd rather read books about regular kids who lose their pet or there's a bully in their class or something. You know, normal stuff.

But who could read on this airplane, anyway? (Besides Jenna.) There was Jack's Game Boy chirping away like a little robot, and "The Farmer in the Dell," and Mrs. Kleenex shrieking and Quinn's *yah-yahs*. I mean, who could concentrate?

The bald guy kept rattling his newspaper and looking at us sideways.

When the seat belt sign got turned off, Mom put Quinn in the aisle. He shot up and down, holding his spider up like an airplane: "BrruuUMMMM!"

Ray joined in with his tractor: "Brummm, rrrRRUUUUMMMMMM . . ."

A lot of passengers reached for their headphones.

When Quinn passed us, Jack grabbed his Spiderplane and held it high. Quinn screamed **SO** loud, like a lady seeing a mouse. "E E E E E E E E !"

"*Spider-Man, my Spider-Man, Spidaspidaspidaspida Spider-Man . . .*" Jack sang.

"E E E E E E E E !"

Even Jenna looked up. "Quinn, jeesh, **STOP!**"

"E E E E E E E E !"

The bald guy slammed his newspaper shut and went to the bathroom.

"Oh, Jack, for heaven's sake!" Mom was on her feet. She took Jack by the arm and put him with Dad and gave Ray to me. Then she took Quinn in her lap and stuck a lollipop in his mouth. He went quiet like Ray's tractor does when you switch it off.

Ray was pretty squirmy after all the excitement, but I gave him my charm bracelet and he calmed down. In the middle of sucking on the silver heart, his head plopped down on my lap and he was asleep. So things were pretty quiet, except for Lily.

"Oh, Mrs. Kleenex, the bad dragon has gone away to a tea party in the ocean!"

I watched the movie for a while. It was about a family with TWELVE children. That's TWO TIMES as many as we have. Wow. Imagine being on an airplane with *them*.

I smooshed my face to the window and looked down. I saw snowy mountains, which meant we were almost there. Gram was probably parking her old gray car right now. I was hoping she'd bring brownies for us, like she did last summer, because I was starving and all I had was a tangerine and a cheese stick.

The mountains got closer.

"One, one thousand, two, one thousand…"
I counted the seconds until we finally
bumped down in Denver. I got up to 1,042.

Chapter 2

Gram looks EXACTLY like Mom but older. I was the first one to spot her in the crowd at the airport. I recognized her hair first. It's poofy and gray, like smoke almost. Then I saw that bright red lipstick she always wears. I rushed over and put my arms around her middle. "Gram!"

"Cleo!"

Up close I could see her dress was covered with little Chinese lanterns.

She kissed me on the cheek. Then she noticed she'd left lipstick marks there. "Oopsy!" She spat in a Kleenex and wiped the spot. I put my hand on my cheek and smiled. Then Jenna and Jack and Ray and everybody came crashing into Gram.

"Okay, everybody gets a big red kiss!" Gram left a trail of lipstick on everybody's cheeks.

"All right, Jenna, you and Cleo take Lily and go with Gram," Dad said when he got the keys to the car. He rented one because there were too many of us to fit in Gram's. The rental was bright blue. I mean, so blue it was funny. It was even funnier when it was packed with three boys and two parents and diapers and bags and all.

"Ha!" Gram laughed. "It looks like the clown car in the circus!"

That's when a small, goofy car comes out stuffed with so many clowns that it seems impossible. They're all sticking out of the windows and yelling at each other and the crowd goes nuts laughing.

Gram's car wasn't so funny. It was just, you know, gray.

The minute me and Jenna were squished in the back next to Lily's car seat, Jenna snapped open her book.

"What's that you're reading, Jen?" Gram asked.

"*Harry Potter.*" Jenna floated right off to wizard land again.

"It's a wizard book," I explained.

"Yes, so I've heard," Gram said. "Have you read it?"

"Nah, I don't like wizard books. Do you?"

"I do, but then I'm a bit of a wizard myself." Gram waved her arms like she was casting a spell. "Watch this: Zing, zang, alacazam!"

I laughed. She looked more like a music conductor than a wizard.

"Presto!" Gram opened the glove compartment: brownies!

"Yes!" I took one and passed the plastic bag to Lily and Jenna. Lily ate her brownie crumb by crumb, singing a song:

"The little red bird eats the little raisins,
then she eats a little worm . . ."

Gram smiled and pulled the old car out onto the busy road.

Gram's house is small and brick and has a special smell, like lamb chops and old furniture. Her kitchen is jammed with food when we come, good things like cinnamon buns and potato chips. She has piles of clean white sheets and we sleep all over the house.

Of course, Jenna took the best bed. It's the one in the guest room, with a pink quilt. I got the trundle under it with the brown, plaid blanket. Plus: 1) **JENNA** got to put cookies in the oven and pass them out at bedtime. And 2) **JENNA** got to call the neighbors back home to see how Lucy was. And 3) **JENNA** got to be in charge of the alarm clock.

"Ahhh, this bed is **SO** cozy," she said when we finally went to bed. She fluffed around in her quilt and poofed her pillows. Then she pulled out that stupid book again.

"Jen, Dad said lights out." My blanket was itchy and my pillow was rubbery and I just wanted to go to sleep.

"One more chapter," Jenna said. Chapters in *Harry Potter* are about a mile long. But I didn't fight about it since fights with Jenna are big and loud and I was just too tired. I pulled the covers over my head.

Sometimes I wish I was a wizard like Harry. I'd make Jenna disappear. *Whoosh*, good-bye, Miss Boss of the World.

Chapter 3

The next day, Mom and Dad packed up the Big Three (me and Jack and Jenna) all over again to go to the mountains for a couple of days. The Little Three were staying with Gram.

"Are you sure you're okay with these monkeys?" Mom asked her.

Quinn was eating Gram's necklace while Ray vroomed around her feet with a toy car.

"Gram dance! Gram dance!" Lily kept begging.

"Piece of cake," Gram said, but she wasn't exactly smiling.

I sat between Jack and Jenna in the car so they wouldn't fight. Jenna read *H.P.* the whole time. I can't read in a car (barf!), so I closed my eyes and pretended the Clown Car was alive.

"Uunnnhhhh . . ." He had to drag us all the way up the mountain to Uncle Chuck's cabin.

"I know you can make it," I said. (In my mind, of course, not out loud.)

"Awwwww . . . oooph." The Clown Car was a real complainer.

About every ten minutes, Jack shouted, "Are we there yet?" just to annoy Jenna.

She was in wizard land, but after about

the eighth "ARE WE THERE YET?" she lost it.

"WILL YOU JUST SHUT UP!?"

"Jack, please," Mom said.

"Are we there yet?" He said it in a tiny girl voice.

Jenna blew. **"Shut up!"**

That was when Dad slammed on the brakes.

"Okay, **knock. It. Off.**" He said it, or yelled it I guess, in that way he has, which pretty much stops all fights fast.

The Clown Car was SO happy to rest for a minute. **"YES!"** he cried.

But a minute later Dad stepped on the gas.

"Noooooooooo," the Clown Car moaned.

When we finally got to the cabin, the Clown Car was panting like our old dog, Lucy. I gave him a pat. "Good job," I said.

"A a a a h h h h h." He went right to sleep.

The cabin was just one big room. It had

two triple bunk beds, a stove and a fridge.
And one mouse, who left really fast.

We had hot dogs and chips and apples
and carrots for supper and Dad told us about
Mount Baldy.

"We'll need an early start tomorrow. It's

fourteen thousand feet high: a big hike. It's like climbing nine Empire State Buildings. Hah!"

I could just see nine buildings on top of each other, all teetering, with us climbing up the sides.

That night I looked out the little window by my bunk and saw about a billion stars. It was like someone threw glitter up at the black sky and it stuck. I tried to count the stars just in one corner of the window, but I fell asleep.

I dreamed I was in a cabin with twelve children and a giant purple spider.

Chapter 4

Dad woke us up like they do in the army. He blew an invisible trumpet:

"Doo, doo, **DOO**DOOdoo, doo DOO **DOO**DOOdoo,

Doo, DOO, **DOO**DOOdoo, doo, **DOOOO**, doo."

He was already dressed. He stretched his arms high. "Uuuuuup!" and then he swung down and touched his toes. "Dooowwwwnn!" Mom joined in while me and Jack and Jenna got some Cheerios. I ate slowly, watching the little circles, all lazy in the milk. They were on vacation, happy as can be. No hiking for them today.

I don't really like hiking all that much. The thing is, Dad forgets that his legs are twice as long as mine. To keep up, I have to move them twice as fast as he moves his.

He'll go **STEP STEP** and I'll have to go stepstepstepstep. So my legs ache like mad.

"OH-kay, let's saddle the horses! Yep!" Dad sure was peppy.

That was just an expression about the horses. I wished we actually had some. We could ride up Mount Baldy, let them do the walking.

The Clown Car took us to the foot of Mount Baldy and I could tell he was happy to stay behind as we headed up the steep path.

Chapter 5

STEP STEP. Stepstepstepstep. I was sweating and panting in about three minutes.

Mom sang her hiking song to keep me going:

> "I think mountain hiking
>   is not to my liking,
> It's not just like climbing up stairs.

It takes a lot longer,

   your legs must be stronger,
And mountains are loaded with bears!"

After about an hour (which seemed like a million years), we stopped for a break.

We were in a meadow that was full of blue flowers and butterflies rushing around. Dad gave each of us a hunk of chocolate from this big, melty bar he carried.

"Don't eat too fast or you'll barf." Jenna licked her chocolate carefully.

"Blaaaaahhhhh!" Jack fake-barfed just to be annoying.

Mom sang her chocolate song:

"Spinach may be full of vitamin E,
But of all vegetables, be suspicious.
For lettuce will lure you,
And carrots will cure you,
But chocolate is much more delicious!"

There was a stream that cut the meadow in half.

"Hey, let's go stream swimming!" I said to Jack.

"Yeah, yeah, yeah, yeah, yeah, yeah, yeah!" Jack started to get undressed. See, we usually

go stream swimming in our underpants, and carry extras to change into after. Of course, if anyone else had been around, like Pete Landon (yikes!) or Flip Bimstein (ick!), I'd never go swimming in my **UNDER-PANTS**. But it was just us, so who cares.

But right when we got our toes wet, a bunch of clouds showed up, moving fast. ZIP, they covered the sun. We put our pants back on and pulled out our jackets.

Jack pretended he was Dad. "Saddle the horses! Up and at 'em!"

Jenna rolled her eyeballs.

We climbed higher, really high.

Chapter 6

We climbed up where the air is thinner, so the trees can't grow. The mountain looked like the bald head of that guy on the airplane; it was all bare on top with scraggly stuff growing around the edges.

More clouds came, a whole crowd of them. They rushed by like they were late for a cloud party. The wind flapped my jacket. I zipped it up all the way.

The path got skinnier and steeper. My dad slipped on the loose rocks.

"Yep, watch your step," he said.

Then I learned what it means when people say the wind whistles, because that's what it started to do. It whistled just like my soccer coach does when you go out of bounds.

"Look at that view, would you? Hah!" Dad stopped us for a minute. We were almost at the top of Mount Baldy.

"I think I see our house!" I really thought I could see all the way to Illinois.

"Cleo, that is so totally not possible." I didn't care what Jenna said. I waved hello to Lucy, back home.

"I can see Egypt!" Jack said, and walked like an Egyptian for about ten minutes, until Jenna yelled at him to stop.

"Say cheese." Dad took pictures of Mom with the mountains behind her.

But she said "Brrrrrrr" instead, and shivered. Then, "Hey!" Mom looked at the sky and held out her hand to catch what fell.

"Oooh!" I felt something wet hit my cheek, right where Gram's lipstick had been.

"SNOW!" Jack shouted. He stuck out his tongue to taste a flake.

"Whoooaaa." Jenna frowned as she watched the snowflakes fall on her blue sleeve.

"Good heavens." Mom laughed for the camera.

Click.

Then it was like some wizard waved a magic wand, the one they use for weather.

Chapter 7

Winter showed up out of nowhere!

It went like this: colder, some snow, REALLY cold, MORE SNOW (not to mention **WIND!**), **FREEZING, LOTS OF SNOW, *BLIZZARD!***

We were in a snowstorm! Just like that!

It was summer! A half an hour ago I was just la-dee-da, my toes in the stream,

and now I was making footprints in snow!

The wind was like a soft wall holding us up, all loud and making our hair crazy. Everything was swirly white.

"Everybody hold hands!" Dad took Jack's hand, Jack took Mom's and I grabbed Mom's jacket and pulled myself close. I turned and reached for Jenna but she just stood there, hugging herself. A tear blew sideways across her cheek.

"Come on, Jen!" I reached harder and grabbed her hand. I had to really pull to get her started.

We found a big rock to huddle next to. I stretched my sleeves down over my hands, but the wind stung my cheeks, like a long slap.

"Here, put these over your heads!" Mom handed us our extra underpants.

I thought about it for a second (EEWWW!) but only a second. Underpants on my head was better than Frosty the Snowman! Me and Jack pulled them on and peeked out through the leg holes.

"I can't, I can't . . ." Mom had to help Jenna with her underpants because she was too shivery and whiny.

"Hee, hee, heeheeheehee hee!" Jack pointed at us and laughed until his pointer finger got too cold and he put it back in his pocket.

Click. Dad took a picture. I thought, *People don't usually stop to take pictures if you're about to freeze to death, so maybe we won't.*

"Are we going to freeze?" I had to kind of yell so Mom could hear me.

"No, honey," she yelled back, and kissed my cold hands.

I just hoped, if we did freeze, nobody would find the camera and the entire world would see pictures of me with underpants on my head.

Jenna was really crying, so Mom put an arm around her. I think maybe Jenna read too much *Harry Potter*, where terrible things happen to kids on every page. She forgot that we're regular children with nice parents and we probably won't die on Mount Baldy, or even get frostbite.

Probably.

Chapter 8

Then the storm got worse.

Dad tucked the camera in his pocket. "Let's walk!" he shouted.

I could hardly hear him now. The wind wasn't whistling anymore, it was kind of screaming. The snow sneaked into my jacket and my socks and pants. I held on tight to Mom and I was just sure Dad could find the way down.

Or pretty sure, anyway.

I was shaking so hard now, it was almost like I was doing some weird dance.

"**Aaaaah!**" Jenna slipped and fell.

Her hand slid out of mine. I pulled on Mom to keep my balance, so then she fell too. Jack yelled to Dad, and they both bent down to help Mom.

Jenna just lay there, all crumpled, like a pile of laundry.

"Get up, Jenna!" I yelled.

"NOOooo, I'm too cold, I'm cold. . . ."

I yelled at her to tuck her legs under, and she did.

"Now hold on!" Her hands were like mine, all red and stiff and wet, and it hurt to grab them. I tried to pull her up, but her legs were all noodly.

"I'm cold, I'm cold . . . ," she kept saying.

"EVERYBODY'S COLD, JENNA! GET UP!" I was totally crabby, but I felt sort of bad for Jenna. She must have been even more freezing and scared than me to let me be so bossy with her.

I got behind her and locked my arms under her armpits. I think suddenly being

the Boss of Jenna made me really strong, because I got her up in one heave: "Uuuup!"

Then Dad and Jack were there. They each took one of Jenna's hands. Mom was back up and we all started walking again. We held on to each other like those elephants you've seen, holding tails with their trunks, all in a line. Even Dad went step . . . step . . . step, just as slow as us.

We inched down Mount Baldy.

Then it was like that wizard waved the Weather Wand again.

Chapter 9

Magically, while we walked, winter just went away, like this: **BLIZZARD**, **SNOW** (not to mention **WIND**), **less wind,** LESS SNOW, CLOUDS LEAVE (underpants come OFF our heads), SUN PEEKS OUT, warmer, warm! And we were back to being a regular family in summer. I let go of Mom's jacket, but Jenna held my hand tight all the way back to the pretty meadow.

When we got there, Jack fake-fainted to the ground. "AAAAaaahhhhhh!"

Then I fell too, and I pulled Jenna down with me. Mom and Dad laughed and fell down, plop, plop, next to us. The grass

smelled like, I don't know, sun. We all just lay there, warm and quiet.

After a while, Mom sang:

"Three bears in a bunch
were out looking for lunch,
When suddenly, Papa Bear said,
'Hey, what's that I'm seeing?
A small human being
With white underpants on her head!'"

Jenna laughed the loudest.

Then I noticed I was really hungry.

"Ham on rye, anyone?" Mom always had extra sandwiches, no matter what.

"Wow," Dad said. "That was something. Hah!"

At first I thought he meant the ham on rye, then I knew he meant the blizzard.

"I get to tell Gram about it," I said. I waited for Jenna to argue, but she didn't. "Jen, you can tell the Little Three."

"'Kay," Jenna said. She was lying on her back, eyes closed.

"I'm going to tell Pete and Flip ALL about it!" Jack announced.

"Jack, DON'T tell about the underpants, okay?" I got all goose bumps just thinking about how embarrassing that would be.

"Aw, that's the best part! They're gonna

love it! Hee, hee, heeheeheeheeHEE!"

I don't think he'll tell. He'll just tease me about it for a million years.

Me and Jack skipped behind Dad all the

way down Mount Baldy. Jenna and Mom followed us slowly back to the Clown Car.

I couldn't wait to tell about our adventure. I could sort of feel the story inside me, like a tiny book, bouncing around while I skipped.

Then I thought about all the other stories I have in there, more tiny books, all in a row. There's the book of when I got stitches in my head. There's one about when Jenna won a toilet seat in the school raffle. There's a little book about when I brought home the school's pet iguana and Jack ran over it with his bike. You know, regular stuff.

But the one from that day on Mount Baldy was different from the others.

Definitely.

I think I might have to call it a wizard book.